To my darling babes—
You are my life's treasure.
May you ever grow in integrity and virtue.

And to Joshua, who loved me.

—MA

For my friends, and my family, and my
future friends, and my future family, and Chewie.

—CN

Text © 2010 Melissa Anderson

Illustrations © 2010 Casey Nelson

Design by Sheryl Dickert Smith

Visit us at ShadowMountain.com

Library of Congress Cataloging-in-Publication Data
Anderson, Melissa.
    The big fib / Melissa Anderson.
        p. cm.
    Summary: A little girl who breaks her mother's cookie jar learns that it is always better to tell the truth and face the consequences than deal with a tiny lie that keeps getting bigger and bigger.
    ISBN 978-1-60641-671-6 (hardbound : alk. paper)
    [1. Stories in rhyme. 2. Honesty—Fiction. 3. Conduct of life—Fiction.] I. Title.
    PZ8.3.A5482Bi 2010
    [Fic]—dc22   2010001336

Printed in China   11/13
RR Donnelley, Shenzhen, China

10 9 8 7 6 5 4 3 2

THE BIG FIB

Written by Melissa Anderson

Illustrated by Casey Nelson

SHADOW
MOUNTAIN

It shattered with a CRASH.

It splintered with a SMASH.

I knew I'd done something I shouldn't have.

MY MOTHER BURST in.

She was shocked.
She was scared.

And when I saw her I knew that she cared.

But I couldn't say what I'd been doing before—
Before she rushed in through the blue kitchen door.

What happened in here?

Her stunned face was white.

"What were you doing? Are you sure you're all right?"

i DiDN'T DO iT!

I said, feeling all sorts of sly.

And that was the start of my gigantic lie.

"I looked way up high, on the very top shelf,

And I saw a small mouse sitting there by himself.

He was pushing and shoving your old cookie jar.

It sat way up high, and it fell very far.

It broke into pieces all over the floor,

But I'm sure with some glue it will look like before."

My mother said **Hmm** and looked
straight in my eyes
And told me that I should never tell lies.
She then shook her head and scratched at her chin,
And spoke without even the tiniest grin—

You had better watch out! The first lie's the trigger.
Your fib will get **BIGGER** and **BIGGER** and **BIGGER.**

I shook in my boots, took a breath, and replied,

i swear it's the truth—
i never would lie!

I'm sure what I told you is just what I saw:

A mouse came out of that
hole in the wall.

He wanted a cookie to eat for his lunch.

He wanted a cookie—something tasty to munch.

I watched him climb to the very top shelf.

It was amazing—he climbed up there all by himself!

He ate all your cookies. He ate every crumb.

He licked up each morsel, and when he was done . . .

COOK

CRASH!
I watched him do it.

BOOM! I think he knew it.

'Cause he stood on that shelf after watching it fall,

And he laughed a big laugh and then hid in the wall.

My mother said **Hmm**

again and again.

She then shook her head and

scratched at her chin,

And spoke without even the tiniest grin—

Remember what I said? The first lie's the trigger.

Your fib will get **BIGGER** and **BIGGER** and **BIGGER.**

I shook in my boots even more than before.

But I couldn't stop now, so

i FiBBeD a BiT MoRe . . .

Eleventeen mouses all leaping about
Ate all your cookies with eleventeen shouts.

They jumped and they scampered around on the floor—
They sommer-ed and sault-ed and swung on the door!

They ate each of your cookies, one after the other,
And before they were done . . . they . . . um . . .

I looked at my mother.

Oh, I nearly forgot—there was one giant rat
Who jumbled on in without stopping to chat.

He stood three feet tall and was round as a berry.
He was fluffy and furry and a little bit hairy.

HE ATE ALL YOUR COOKIES

(every last one)
And sauntered away when they were all gone.

If it were me, I'd be downright impressed,
'Cause it was your cookies that
he liked the best.

Mother just looked at me straight in the eyes.
I knew in my heart **she** would never tell lies.
I was feeling so guilty my face turned bright red.
It made me ashamed where my big fib had led.

SO i CONFESSED.

I wanted a cookie. I knew that I shouldn't.
I tried to be good. It's just that I couldn't.
I pulled up a chair. I did it myself.
I climbed way up high to the very
top shelf.

i ATE ALL THE COOKIES AND THEN TOLD YOU A LIE.

Now I feel sorry and

JUST WANT
TO CRY.

My mother then gave me the tightest embrace

And wiped all the tears away from my face.

She told me, "I'm sorry for the lie that you chose,

But now you know well how a fib like that grows.

There is an effect for every small deed,

And this was a lesson I knew that you'd need."

So today I'm outside, just weeding the yard,

Earning some money for a new cookie jar.

I'm replacing the cookies—the broken jar, too—

As I learn the importance of actions I choose.

I've learned a big lesson about fibbing today.

I will never tell lies—it's the truth I will say!

I will shake my head and scratch at my chin

And tell the truth again and again.

From this moment on I won't be a fibber,

'Cause fibs just get

BiGGER

and

BiGGER

and

BIGGER